"This lyrical novel immediately voices layers of spirituality that are so familiar to those who, like the author, have worked intimately with dying individuals and their families.. Important narrative themes such as 'willingness versus willfullness' are explored while the underlying message gradually emerges that unity with greater wholeness is the lens through which we all must thrive. I can't wait for the next in this new series!"

— Ty Clement, Therapist and author of *Being Ourself*

ANGEL OF PROMISE

A NOVEL

BY
SAM OLIVER

Blessings!

Sam Oliver

Dedicated to:

Rosa Lee Johnson

Other Books by Sam Oliver include:

A Fish Named Ed

God a Logs on Living and Dying

The Path into Healing

Another Path into Healing

What the Dying Teach Us: Lessons on Living

Contents

History of Promise Angels

*O*ver 3,000 years ago, Angels of Promise lived *with humans to remind them of the promises they made at birth. The angels would remain near the human until each promise was completed. It was a time of spiritual development enabling humans to reach their full potential. The angels lived somewhere between heaven and earth in a place much like the Garden of Eden. The plant life was lush, green, and filled with endless energy radiating in and through the foliage surrounding them all. It was a peace filled place where everything needed was present in abundance.*

In this place, humans were being prepared to take the place of the Promise Angels assigned to them. This

1

allowed the Promise Angels to leave their place in the world and move on to higher realms in the Kingdom of Heaven. This created an eternal relationship between the angel and human beings that would link their particular growth into experiencing and expressing their soul's deepest longings to reveal oneself.

Promise Angels had a specific purpose to fulfill in the lives of the relationships they were connected to during their partner's path into enlightenment. Their purpose was to love unconditionally their mate and help him or her grow into their most authentic self. Such non-judgmental relating between their angel and human being enabled the human to explore regions of the universe until he or she found the path they were meant to fulfill in this lifetime. It led the human being into a path of peace and enough love to last a lifetime.

This movement into higher and higher awareness of one's most authentic self meant being true to who you really are in order for the next step into eternal relationships to forge a connection between heaven and earth. Thus, the relationship between humans and angels began a journey into the divine aspects of living powered by the desire to connect with an entity deep within oneself.

It allowed the ego to be subdued and the spiritual side of humanity to achieve awareness of its true nature.

One day, a man wanted to be a full fledged human responsible for his own growth without having to take the journey alongside an angel he was dependent on for his movement into the heavenly realms. His desire distorted the creative order. An angelic council met to determine the course of history. They decided to give this man a choice. Left to himself, this man chose to enter his path into humanity of his own accord.

A wise elderly angel made one addendum to this choice. The elderly angel created birth promises and occasional visits from his Promise Angel that would begin at mid-life. When a human being made choices that would inevitably lead to his or her own demise, their angel of promise would appear in their lives and offer a path into one's most authentic self and give guidance into a healing path. And thus, a new world order began.

The Journey into Soul

The night had fallen upon the day's illumination of the sun. Spring had given way to summer creating summer nights that revealed the stars both near and far lighting up the darkness. Silence began to overtake the day's chattering filled with events of the day and the days yet to be. All had gone to bed except Lee, who was watching TV on the couch in the living room until he could no longer keep his eyes open. As usual, there was nothing but senseless bufoonery in lieu of any kind of decent programming. No wonder they called it the "boob tube" Lee thought. He always marveled that our modern technology could be wasted on such meaningless drivel. Yet it did function as an effective sleep aid, as it failed to hold his attention and instead made his eyelids feel leaden. As Lee grew more and more drowsy on the couch, the night air from the window open next to him lulled him into a deep sleep. Soon he was snoring quietly, lost in his own unconscious world of thoughts and dreams.

As Lee and the rest of the family slept, the front door crashed opened somewhere long after the stroke of midnight and awakened Lee's wife Rose who was upstairs sound asleep in bed. The house's peaceful silence was shattered by a terrifying noise. A petite, highly spirited Swedish woman with curly blond hair and delicate features. Rose dashed down the stairs and into the living room shouting, "What's going on?"

She arrived just in time to see Lee confronting a man wearing a ski mask and carrying a flashlight. The man turned to run out the same door he'd just entered by when Lee tackled him. A loud struggle ensued and the two exchanged blows for what in reality was only about ten seconds but felt like ten hours to Lee. He hadn't been in an actual fistfight since elementary school, and this intruder was stronger and apparently younger than Lee. But the guy was clearly terrified of being caught and fought like a wildcat as the two men went at it like a couple of heavyweight boxers.

With his adrenaline pumping, Lee was actually winning the battle with this desperate criminal, getting in a number of hard punches. But then his assailant seemed to remember the flashlight he was carrying and cracked Lee over the head with it. Lee let go of the man and rolled on the carpet in pain, holding his head tightly with both hands. He saw stars in front of his eyes as the unwelcome visitor fled out the door and into the night.

Meanwhile, Rose had dialed 911 and the police were already on their way. They arrived within minutes, their blaring sirens waking up the quiet neighborhood. Lee was now sitting on the couch, shaking and on edge after what had just happened. His head still hurt like hell, though his vision had returned to normal now. It all seemed like a dream, a nightmare, an other worldly event that had broken up a peace filled night.

Rose had planned a trip with their daughters for months, to go visit her sister who lived down in Florida, and they were scheduled to leave in a few days. The police suggested that they begin that trip now. "Kids get really traumatized by this kind of stuff," one of two responding officers, a heavyset older guy with a thick black moustache, explained. Lee agreed that it was a good idea.

"But I don't want to leave you here," Rose said to her husband after the police had left and they had managed to calm their daughters down enough to get them back to bed.

"I think it would be best," Lee insisted. "The girls might be sort of creeped out here in the house for a while. You heard what that cop said."

His wife didn't put up much more of an argument and agreed. In a way, Lee was actually a bit disappointed. He thought maybe she'd want to cancel the trip and be with him after such a frightening incident. But the truth was, they hadn't been getting along very well in recent days and maybe she just wanted to get away from him for awhile to think things through. Of course, that didn't make him feel any better about them and their relationship.

Rose and their three girls hit the road early in the morning. In shock and anger at the same time, Lee reflected on the night's events with much dismay as he sat at the kitchen table sipping coffee in the silence. The clock ticking quietly on the wall was the only sound. Lost in thought, Lee wondered what kind of future he was headed into. He had been laid off from his job a few months ago and with the bad economy his prospects of finding a new job seemed bleak. But it was more than just the financial hardship that was gnawing at his insides like an angry hamster. Much of Lee's self-esteem had been derived from how his job sustained his family, and he worried about how the family would view him now that he was unemployed. *They're probably already thinking of me as a loser*, he mused.

And that's exactly how he felt about himself at this very moment. What kind of a man sits around the house all day and collects an unemployment check instead of going out into the world and working to support his family? Lee laughed bitterly as he realized he had turned into exactly the kind of a guy he had always criticized. A loafer. A slacker. A loser.

Lee grew up as a preacher's son with strong values, first and foremost of which were working hard for your family, purity, and respect. His present situation was not the kind of world that Lee had ever envisioned for himself. He knew that circumstances had been thrust upon him that were beyond his control. Lee was the exact opposite of lazy and in fact in some might have branded him a workaholic. Still, in his mind not working was not working. Lee was the kind of man who defined himself and his value as a human being by his willingness to work hard and to bring home a paycheck large enough to take care of all the needs of his family. Now he was struggling just to get by – and things would only go from bad to worse when his unemployment benefits ran out. They might even lose their house! He placed his elbows on the table and lowered his forehead into his palms. Despondent, he found himself hating the world that he lived in and no longer even knew his place in it. It seemed as though the world Lee had tried so hard to create his entire life no longer existed.

After pondering these things throughout the day, he grew tired and sleep overtook him again. He wrestled with his pillow for hours until finally drifting off into a fitful slumber. During his sleep, a bright yellow glow appeared to him. It made his eyes feel warm and peace filled his body like a tranquil stream, diverting his attention into an endless penetrating flow of energy cleansing his entire being. In the distance, an angel appeared to be walking on a path that led directly toward him.

But was it an angel? How was he to know? After all, he'd never seen an angel before. Yet, somehow, he was certain of it. Something beyond his five senses confirmed that his instinctual conjecture was undoubtedly correct.

Lee found himself facing a figure in front of him and felt as though he'd known this personage all his life. He was not afraid, but Lee welcomed this presence. Kindness emanated from this angelic being. Lee embraced the tranquil experience – such a stark contrast to the violent turmoil from the previous night that he wished to forever purge from his memory.

"Hello," Lee said to the figure in front of him.

"Hello," came the reply.

"Who are you?" Lee inquired.

"I am an angel here to remind you who you are."

"What is your name?" asked Lee, befuddled.

"My name is "Promise.""

"What are you doing here?" Lee said.

"I am here to help you remember something," the angel said.

"What would that be?"

"I am here to help you remember the promises you made to me the moment you were born," the angel answered.

Now Lee was perplexed. "What promises are you talking about?"

"When you were born, I appeared to you much like I am doing now. What happened was that you promised to fulfill seven missions for me, and I promised to be with you through them all with a promise of my own to you. I promised to follow you through life and help you stay focused on fulfilling those seven promises you made during your entrance into what you call earth. You are now at a crossroads in your life, and I am here to help you fulfill a destiny you were born to live," said the angel.

Lee had been listening carefully to every word that Promise had uttered. As incredible as all of this seemed, he also had to admit that it made a lot of sense. He asked, "This destiny wouldn't have anything to do with me seemingly failing to live up to those promises right now would they?"

"Ha, ha, ha…my friend…you could never fail to live up to who you are even if you tried," the angel said with a chuckle.

"I don't get what you mean," Lee said. "Look at me now. I have failed. I am not even good at being a family man nor anything else I have tried to this point. I haven't succeeded in a way that I had hoped many years ago."

The angel took a deep sigh and said, "You measure your success and failure by what you have done or not done. I tell you, and never forget this my friend. The measure of a man is not in whether he perceives himself to be a success or not. Instead, the measure of a man's success is determined by his ability to hold on to the promises he makes to his angel the moment he is born."

This was intriguing. It was the first time Lee had heard any of this. Or was it? Maybe this was something that he'd known all of his life – but had now somehow forgotten about it. "Did you make a promise to me?" Lee wanted to know. "And did I make a promise to you?"

"All in good time, my friend, all in good time," the angel whispered.

The night's dream faded into the night just like it came into being. Lee wanted to know more, and tried to keep the dream alive. But dreams just don't work that way. They take on a life of their own, and the dreamer does not control them. There's no remote control button to manipulate what happens, no matter how much we might want there to be.

Lee awakened to a new day. He had no idea what he was going to do. He didn't know whether to stay or leave. The empty house felt like it was closing in on him. The marital problems that Lee and his wife had been experiencing, along with his jobless situation, had sank his heart to new depths of despair.

"I've got to get out of here," he finally said to nobody but the four walls. He decided to get his life in order by taking some time away from the family to think. All Lee knew was that he wanted to find a place he could call home. But where would he go?

The entire day seemed like a coma. He was alive, but he was not awake to the world around him. Lee contemplated what to do until he realized he needed to return to a place he knew he would be accepted with unconditional love. There was only one place that would meet that criteria.

On his third day alone, Lee packed his bags and drove to Kentucky to live with his family. It took two days to reach the Bluegrass state. Lee took his time leaving Ohio, driving through Indiana, and eventually making his way into the Commonwealth of Kentucky, where he was born. All he could think during his many hours on the road was how he had not lived up to the expectations he had of himself as a father and a husband. "What went wrong?" he said to himself over and over.

As Lee passed by the "Welcome to Kentucky" sign on the Interstate, memories of his childhood flooded his mind. He fondly recalled the day he bought his first car. It was a yellow Ford Mustang. He was so proud of his new shiny car. It belonged to Lee, and he felt so independent and powerful. Occasionally, Lee would race his new car with his buddy Dana who had an 8 cylinder engine in his GTO. Dana would always win until one fateful night. Lee's 4 cylinder engine seemed to have power beyond any other day or night Lee had known. On this night, Lee's yellow Mustang became known as "the yellow streak" because this was all Dana could see as Lee's car roared past him like he was standing still. The memories just came streaming back to him as though Lee was being filled with a new energy and a new life to create in the days ahead.

Lee stayed a couple of days with his family. It was good to see his mom and dad, his sister and her husband, and his brother and his family. He had some good home cooking, and especially savored the deep fried biscuits he had always loved so much as a boy. Him and his brother even had some fun tossing the football around in the backyard just like in the old days.

On the third day of his visit, Lee asked his dad if Grandpa's cabin still resided in the woods near "The Garden of the Gods."

"I believe so, Lee" said Dad.

"Do you still have the keys to the old cabin?" Lee asked.

"I believe I do, son."

"I need to take some time away and be to myself this summer. I've been through a lot and I need to get my head clear," Lee explained.

But there was no need to have to explain anything. His father smiled. "I understand," he said. "Take your time up there. Your grandpa once said that on long summer nights he could hear the wind talk to him."

"Thanks Dad. I will need to listen to something other than the words I keep hearing in my own head."

Dad just laughed at his son, put his arm around his shoulder and said, "Don't leave that mountain until you hear the voice of your soul, and then, you will be ready to live and live life without fear."

Lee pondered these words as he packed his car and drove down the road to the Illinois state line to board a ferry leaving Kentucky and crossing the river into Illinois where Grandpa's cabin was. There weren't a lot of fellow passengers on the ferry that day, but even if there were Lee wouldn't have noticed them. He'd become completely absorbed into his own thoughts, his own problems.

As the slow moving boat crossed the river dividing Kentucky and Illinois, Lee stared into the murky water's dark depths. He remembered some of the stories Grandpa told him as a small child about the Garden of the Gods. He once told Lee that he heard an angel's voice in those hills. After many days alone in those hills, Grandpa said that a man could hear things in the spiritual world like no other place on earth. He once declared that he even caught the vision of an angel appearing before him in a splendid white robe and a golden light that lit up the darkness around them.

Those stories had always fascinated Lee as a child, and for a long time he believed every word of them as literally true. But as he grew older and became more educated, developing into an adult, he became skeptical. Things such as angels and spirits, he became convinced, were for the gullible and the naïve. Surely his grandfather was just a kindly old man who liked to tell nice stories to children. But none of these tales could actually be true.

Or could they? After that vivid dream he'd had the other night, Lee wasn't so sure anymore. The "rational" part of him kept making sobering arguments. It was just the result of all of the stress from the intruder. It had something to do with all of the problems he'd been having with Rose. It was the result of his terrible unemployment situation making him feel guilty and therefore conjuring up this imaginary angel.

After a while, Lee had enough of all of this self psychoanalyzing. Maybe there was no good psychological explanation for it. Maybe dreams just happen. They're figments of our imagination and as such defy all attempts to fully understand them.

Of course, that line of reasoning would only satisfy Lee for a short while. The dream was too vivid for him to just dismiss it so easily. Maybe there was more to the world than meets the eye.

Once in Illinois, Lee drove off of the boat and through the small city on the other side of the river and into the hills on a single lane road that became more winding and more bumping with every passing mile. He drove for well over an hour through acres and acres of forest climbing higher and higher terrain with each mile. The road leading to the Garden of the Gods had many curves and plant life everywhere in sight. Along the way, Lee slowed down for a family of deer to cross the road ahead of him. They looked sharply and quickly at him as though he was invading their territory.

Eventually, Lee made it to the Garden of the Gods. There was a cleared out area of gravel for parking. He stepped out of his car and followed the trail leading into the woods ahead of him. Serenely hiking without another human in sight, Lee eventually reached the highest point of the trail and looked over the boulders of rock embedded into the earth's crust. Below this mountainous panorama was a valley so deep that he could not see the bottom. It was as he remembered as a child when his Grandpa took him into the woods to show him the natural beauty of God's creation. The same wonder that filled his spirit all those many years ago swept over him now once again, and he stood there for so long taking it all in that he lost track of time. H did, however, notice that the sun had sunk a bit in the western sky. And the warm breeze picked up slightly too.

When he finally tore himself away from gazing into the abyss, Lee decided to return to the car and pull out his camping gear to hike his way to the old cabin deep in the woods. Along the way, Lee saw squirrels, more deer, birds, and snakes. Each step of the way was natural formations of rocks, forests, and animals that had made a home in those hills where few humans even wanted to travel. Lee was fascinated by each event taking place in front of him. His attention turned from the worries of the world to an inner appreciation of the world around him. He walked the rest of the afternoon and into the night.

As he walked along the trail, Lee purposely refused to entertain any thoughts of worry or strife. All of that would have to wait for another day. For now, it was time to simply enjoy his surroundings and absorb all of the natural goodness of this place into his soul. Every breath seemed more than just air to him. Not only was it more pure, it seemed to have a soothing quality about it that made him appreciate every instance of filling up his lungs, briefly holding it in, and then letting it out again. *Sort of like life*, he thought with a chuckle. *Take in what's good and hold it for as long as you can, then realize that there's also some stuff in your life that's no good for you and just let it go.* Maybe this little trip would help him to distinguish between the two.

Finally, he reached the cabin Grandpa had told him about as a small boy. It was much smaller than he had imagined. Lee stepped onto the small porch with a small roof hanging over his head and opened the door in front of him. It creaked from years of non-use. When he stepped into the cabin, it was filled with dust that has been sitting there untouched for who knew how many years.

Talk about humble! The cabin was a single room with a toilet on one side of the room with a torn curtain that circled around it. A single bed occupied the other corner, and there was a small wood stove in the center of the room for heating and cooking. The log cabin was not much bigger than the living room in his home in Ohio. It didn't matter to Lee. This was home.

The first week was spent remembering the events that had led Lee to this place. Emotions ranged from extreme anger to profound joy. It was as though Lee was walking through a mine field not knowing if the next step would explode into an emotion he wanted so desperately to forget. The nights were calmer for Lee. At least, he could sleep soundly with the crickets drowning out the chattered voices haunting his past.

One thing he was sure of: life never turns out exactly the way you plan it. In fact, it wasn't all that long ago that Lee had thought that he'd had it all figured out. He had a stable job, a good income, a happy marriage and healthy, well-adjusted kids. But then he lost his job, he and his wife began to argue about money and a dozen other things, and Lee started questioning every decision that he had never made.

Maybe I was married too young. Maybe she was too young. Maybe we both were. After all, we were immature and thought that it was the right thing to do because we were in love. And there's no denying that we were. Not only that, we still love each other even now, even after the fighting and the bitter words. But could it be that we're just not a good match? Maybe we don't belong together. Maybe we should have taken more time so that we could both see other people and get to live the single life rather than getting married at 21 years old.

These thoughts kept nagging at Lee day after day as he re-assessed the decisions that had brought him to this point in his life.

Rose is a wonderful woman, but I wonder if she really does love me as much as I love her. I mean, she tells me that she loves me all the time, but I wonder if those are just words? Wonder if she says it just to keep the peace? Does she really want to be with me, or is she staying with me just for the sake of the kids? Does she plan on leaving me when they grow up and leave the house?

Lee hated questioning his wife like this. She had never given him any reason for him to be so suspicious. He was certain that she had always been faithful to him, as he had been to her. Yet...those dreadful worries persisted and hounded him. He wanted to chase them away, but each time they ran right back into his thoughts, along with other bouts of second guessing everything from his choice of a career to the size of the house that they bought. He finally came to the conclusion that second guessing could drive a man out of his mind.

The second week was much calmer. Lee found himself listening to the sounds of nature and allowing the earth's vibrations and rhythms to soothe his heart. This nurturing of Lee's heart moved his attention into the essence of creation. He found himself listening to sounds created by nature; instead of the sounds of a hustle and bustle world where stress creates the world around you and inside you. Lee began to allow life to reveal itself to him. In so doing, Lee was connecting to a world much larger than he could imagine in the material world a city provided. It was as though Lee was experiencing the world moving through him and not from him. In essence, Lee realized he was a part of the whole of creation and not separated from it.

By the time the third week came along, Lee was in unity consciousness. He no longer believed himself to be a unique individual living in the world. He believed himself to be completely integrated into a fabric of living called life. The Lee known in Ohio no longer existed. Lee just experienced himself as One presence in touch with it all.

This completely changed his perspective on things. No longer did he waste time worrying about his problems because he came to understand that, in reality, there were no problems. In nature, all is good. Things just are, because they are supposed to be. A tree has no problems, nor does a deer or a fish. They just live because they were created by God to live. They were given life, and they simply live that life rather than go through the life they have been given worrying about things that they cannot change. It's a lesson that human beings need desperately to learn, but seldom do.

Each day became an adventure to Lee. He noticed everything in the woods like he had never noticed them before. The sounds of nature were clearer to him, and he swore at times that he could hear the wind speak to him.

One sunny afternoon he was out by the side of the trail gathering berries when a small sound tickled his ears.

"Hello."

"What was that?" Lee said.

"Hello, Lee."

Lee was startled for a moment, but his openness to nature revealing life to him made him grow in confidence of his ability to experience things in this new terrain. Rather than fear whatever it was that was speaking to him, Lee was intrigued by it. He did his best to listen for it again, but the voice did not return.

He didn't hear this sound the rest of the day.

When the day came to a close, Lee was tired. He walked back to his cabin to eat the blackberries he'd found on the trail earlier that day. The summer night was clear and the stars pierced their way through the tree leaves illuminating the cabin with natural light. Lee sat on the porch before retiring for the night and just took time to listen again for the voice he'd heard in the woods earlier that day. All he could hear was the leaves stirring in the night from the wind.

The next day brought new adventures unlike the day before. Lee found a stream of water and carved out a stick until a sharp point came forth, making it possible to catch a fish in this creek bed about a mile from his cabin. There were sections of this stream that made the waters look white as it toppled over the rocks below it. Here, trout were making their way up the stream to find a mate to fill the stream with more of its kind. They were everywhere and Lee had no trouble catching three huge fish for dinner that night. His mouth salivated at the prospect of a tasty dinner that he'd sear in a frying pan over the open fire.

Lee put a few logs in the stove centered in the middle of the cabin, so he could cook the fish in the frying pan he found in his Grandpa's cabinets. It didn't take long for the stove to heat up and those three fish to find a new home in Lee's stomach. After eating to fulfillment, Lee walked outside to sit on the porch and just savor the night air. The breeze was stirring mildly, and he could hear the tree limbs in the forest rubbing against one another as though they were all a part of an orchestra playing a melody never heard before. Lee was content in a way he had not been in a long time. He did not have trouble going to sleep that night.

The next morning, Lee took a hike on a path he had not yet traveled. He walked for some time noticing all the ferns and wildflowers along the way. Ahead he heard a sound much like a waterfall. His Grandpa had told him of this waterfall. It was a place of mystery and a place he used to go to bathe. As he approached it, there was green moss and rock formations everywhere. He remembered Grandpa telling him there was a hidden passageway behind the waterfall that led into a cave. Was that just another one of his grandfather's stories, or was there some truth to it? When the time was right, Lee decided that he would have to find out for himself.

The waterfall was indeed beautiful and flowing well from the rainfall during the night. Lee just had to jump in for a swim and a cleaning. He took his shoes, shirt, and pants off. It was cold, but Lee's naked body adapted to it soon enough. He relaxed in the fresh cool water for some time just soaking it all in. Then, he remembered what Grandpa had told him about the cave. Lee dipped his head into the water and dove as deep as he could. On his first attempt, he kept running into a wall of rock formations. On his second attempt, he breathed in until his lungs were filled to capacity, and then he dove deeper, much deeper, and found an opening that he swam into daring to discover what his Grandpa had promised.

When Lee surfaced to the other side, he found himself inside the cave that Grandpa had spoke about. It was dark, but there were small openings that reflected on the crystals inside lighting up every corner of the cave. Lee felt intrigued by this discovery. His heart felt like a small boy's heart anticipating his first Christmas gift and what lay deep inside it. His eyes gazed across the room as his mouth was open in awe of the moment. Then, he heard it again.

"Hello."

"Who is that?" said Lee, looking in all directions but seeing nothing.

"It's me."

Lee spoke with authority and a little nervous since he had no clothes on. "Show yourself," he insisted.

"You're not ready." The voice faded into the cave as quickly as it appeared. He strained to hear it again, but his efforts were in vain.

Lee had heard this voice before, but he could not recall where. It sounded like a voice calling him to a place remembered from long ago. He even wondered if it was Grandpa trying to contact him. A lot of strange things had happened to him in the weeks he'd been up here, but that would be just too difficult to believe.

After a few more moments, Lee decided that there was no reason to stay in the cave for any longer right now. So he dove into the water again and swam through its cold depths to the other side of the cave and walked back to Grandpa's cabin after getting dressed.

On the way home, Lee gave thought to this voice calling for his attention. "What is going on?" Lee said to himself. By this point, he was beginning to miss conversations with his wife and family. Being in nature has its own communication, but he missed sharing words with other human beings, his wife most of all. What was it about human conversation and the human voice that was so special? He smiled as he imagined what it must have been like to have been Adam before the creation of Eve.

That night, Lee was restless for the first time since he'd been sleeping in Grandpa's cabin. In fact, he could not sleep. After while, he gave up and simply gazed at the ceiling with his eyes wide open.

Then, he heard that voice again. "Lee."

"Yes," Lee said.

"You're ready now," said the voice.

"For what?" Lee asked.

"To see and talk to me," said this soft deep voice.

"Who are you?" Lee said.

There was no immediate answer.

"Who are you?" Lee said again, this time his voice more insistent.

"I am an angel. My name is Promise."

"Let me see you," Lee said, realizing he'd heard that name before. "Have you been speaking to me for some time?"

"Yes," said the angel.

"What do you want of me?" Lee exclaimed, wondering why, if this truly was an angel, he had decided to contact him.

"I want you to remember something. I want you to remember when you first saw me," the angel's voice faded into the night.

Lee had so many questions that he wanted to ask. But the angel had apparently left. Was this just a dream? Was he trying so hard to fall asleep that he did fall asleep, and now he had dreamed of this angel? Just like that other dream he'd had? Could he be hallucinating?

As Lee pondered these things, he fell into a deep sleep this time. He began to dream about events in his life that were important to him, but his life-span was remembered backwards in time. He remembered all the way back to the moment he was born. During the moment he was being born, Lee remembered speaking to an angel and making seven promises to this angel that he would fulfill in his lifetime. When he looked at the angel in his dream, it awakened him from a sound sleep. He couldn't make out who this angel was, but he had a familiar look about him. Slowly, Lee opened his eyes in the cabin's darkened room. As he looked the room over, Lee noticed a glow at the cabin's door. The door began to open and the glow of a man stood at this door calling for Lee. Lee yelled out, "Who are you? What do you want?"

"I am the one you just dreamed about."

"This has to be a dream," Lee said to himself.

"I assure you, you are no longer dreaming, Lee. I am an Angel of Promise. I am here to help you fulfill the promises you made to me at birth and to fulfill the one promise I made to you."

"Have you been following me all this time?" Lee wanted to know.

"Yes, but I could not reveal myself until you were ready."

"But, you look like an ordinary man," Lee stated.

"I am appearing to you this way because you would not accept me any other way," explained the angel. "I can assure you that I am the angel you have heard whisper to you in your dreams in the night and the day."

"Ok, prove it," Lee challenged.

Everything inside of him was instinctively telling Lee that this was true. He could detect absolutely nothing deceitful or untrue about this person. Yet that skeptical part of him continued to make its demands, against his better judgment.

"You were born in Russellville, Kentucky, May 26, 1962," the angel said without hesitation. He didn't seem to mind or take any offense at being questioned at all. To the contrary, he was quite cheerful as he proceeded to share into the night about Lee's parents and siblings as though he knew them personally.

After a long night of listening to his life story from birth until the present day, Lee was convinced that an angel really was appearing to him in physical form. The angel was a strong medium sized man with a beard and curly brown hair. An ordinary figure, a plain and simple man. The angel talked to him all through the night.

The angel told Lee that he had to go the next morning, but he would be back to help him fulfill his seven promises he made to him at birth. Lee began to realize why this cabin in the Garden of the Gods was so important to Grandpa. Grandpa used to go there every summer. He would come back with some wild stories. Grandma thought he had lost his mind, but Lee and the other grandchildren would listen for hours. Lee now felt connected to Grandpa in a way he never had before. He realized that Grandpa was sharing more than stories with his grandchildren. He was sharing his soul.

Come to think of it, the angel looked a lot like Grandpa, but something was different than how he remembered him. Grandpa died years ago at the age of 96. He lived a long life working on a farm in Western Kentucky. He and Grandma were married over 77 years. They met and married at an early age. Grandpa used to give rides to his grandchildren on a bull that was very tame, so the grandkids could tell their friends about it. He used to let them drive his tractor and they all promised not to tell their parents. He was fun and full of natural wisdom he shared through stories.

Lee realized he needed to sleep part of the morning, or he would not be able to sleep that night. He was very tired, and slept through the morning and into the early evening hours. When he woke up, he couldn't believe he had slept so much during the day. "Oh well," he said, "this is going to be a long night."

Lee decided to make a fire outside his cabin that night to ponder what the angel had shared with him. He wondered how someone that looked like a man could claim to be an angel and know the things he did in great detail about his entire life. Who could know him so well?

Maybe it is Grandpa, he thought. Could Grandpa have faked his death and returned to the mountains here to stay and is simply looking much younger these days? This couldn't be it, he said to himself. Lee had no way to explain away what had just happened to him. This angel must be real. It was then that Lee realized when the angel revealed himself more boldly. It was after Lee's visit to the cave of crystals in The Garden of the Gods.

The following day, Lee set out to remember the seven promises he made to this angel the moment he was born. He also wanted to remember what promise this angel made to him when he was born. It was such an other worldly experience for Lee that he could hardly believe this was happening to him.

I Promise to Remember

The morning came early for Lee, and he recalled a time in his life during high school. It was his senior year. He remembered feeling sad about leaving his family, friends, and a small town named Marion that he had come to love in Western Kentucky. The people were laid back and very religious for the most part. There was a church on almost every street. Everyone knew everyone in that town.

It was the day of Lee's graduation. The high school was packed full of family members and friends attending the graduation ceremony of the Crittenden County High School. Lee remembered walking up front to receive his diploma and a deep sadness came over him. It felt as though he was saying goodbye to a world he had come to know and love. Life would never be the same, Lee thought. He would no longer be surrounded by the friends he had made over the course of four years. Their support and love for Lee had sustained him and he would miss it. It felt as though the bottom of living had fallen out from under him. Lee had become a part of the basketball, cross country, and track teams. The encouragement for Lee to excel in being the best he could be touched his heart.

Lee was going to attend college that fall. It was a new adventure and the first time in his life that he would experience a world apart from his mom and dad. He discovered that he could make new friends and find new experiences that would enhance his life for years to come. The young man was learning to make the most of the moments he had with those who were presently in his life.

On one of his walks through the woods, Lee found what looked like a tree house. There was a rickety wooden ladder nailed to the side of the huge tree. Lee tested out the rungs and they felt secure, so gingerly he began to climb towards the top. Halfway up he felt one of the rungs begin to give way, but he scrambled up to the next rung without a problem and soon he popped his head up through a creaky trapdoor made of plywood and he was inside.

He looked around the surprisingly large structure and was immediately struck by how much hard work somebody — most likely kids — had put into this place. There were funny, cartoon-like drawings in multiple colors of paint on the walls, carefully carved out windows and even crude furniture. Lee knew how wet these woods get during the rainy season that would have deluged the tree house each year, yet the interior of this place was remarkably dry. He examined it further and saw that somebody had covered the thatched roof with pine tar pitch, making an excellent sealant.

Lee sat down on a bench that had been nailed to the floor and fashioned into a sort of a "couch" by the addition of several fluffy pillows. He leaned back, put his hands behind his head and said, "Ah the good life." Though somebody else had built this place, he assumed they wouldn't mind that it was now providing rest and relaxation for a total stranger.

The thought made Lee wonder about who had built this place. Even without the cartoon-like drawings, something told him that it must have been built by kids. Probably decades ago. Could it have been Grandpa when he was a boy? There was no way to know for sure. During their many conversations, his grandfather had never mentioned anything about a tree house. Then again, this was very deep in the woods, far off the beaten path. Perhaps it was meant to be a secret? Maybe the idea was that the privilege of enjoying this remarkable tree house would be granted only to those who took the time to find it. This was just nothing but idle speculation and conjecture, of course, but Lee liked the idea.

It also took his mind back to his own childhood. He fondly recalled how he and his brother and sister had made one in their back yard growing up. The floor had a hole to climb through for two people to sleep. Or, there was enough room for four people to sit and talk. It was small, not nearly as elaborate as the structure he was currently in, but a point of pride nonetheless for all three siblings. It was a shared accomplishment, something that they had been able to do by putting their heads together and cooperating to fulfill a common purpose. They didn't care a whit whether it was small or big, simple or complex. There was no competition, no zeal to "one up" anybody. How different from the jaded person he had somehow become later in life. Maybe that happens to everyone. Maybe we forget how to just appreciate what it is that we have in life and how all that we need to do is to live in the present moment.

Lee thought about that for a moment. It had been so easy to join together in a spirit of helpfulness just for the sheer fun of it when he was a child. They didn't even have to give it a second thought. These things, like everything else, just came naturally. There were no ulterior motives. Nobody was trying to make money. There were no long-term plans, no worries about who would get the credit. They simply decided one day that it would be really cool to build a tree house, so they set out to make their dream become a reality. Never was there any thought of failure. There was no one claiming that the job would be impossible, that building a tree house would be too difficult. Children, he realized, don't think that way. This doesn't happen until we "grow up."

Smiling at the thought, Lee wondered what it was that made people lose their sense of innocence and openness that seems to come so easily to children. *When did it happen to me?* he pondered. *When did I decide that it mattered what people thought about me? Why do perceptions matter more than reality? How did I become so blind to what truly matters in life?*

There were many times when Lee and his brother would challenge each other to races though. Lee could run much longer than his brother, but his brother could easily zip past him in short runs, leaving him in the dust. It never made Lee angry, though, because it seemed like, despite their boyish arguments sometimes, he and his brother would always end up laughing and having a good time. In fact, they often got so silly when playing together that it would last long into the evening when their mother would finally have to come upstairs and, inevitably, say, "OK, you two clowns, the circus is over. Time for bed." When the boys would loudly protest, her retort was always the same, "You always have tomorrow."

Lee was closest to his brother, but he had a good relationship with his sister too. They learned to play the piano together, and would spend many hours sitting side by side on the old piano bench practicing until both of them had developed into quite skillful pianists. The image of he and his sister at one of their many piano recitals stood firmly fixed in his mind's eye. How long has it been since I've gone near a piano? Lee thought. When he got married and bought his own house he considered buying a piano and keeping up with his music, as it had become very important to him. Yet, somehow, other things were always more important. There was always some other pressing need that required the money. Lee had come to think of things such as buying a piano as "frivolous" and a waste of time and money for a father with children to raise. How many other dreams had he allowed to wither and die?

As he reclined some more on the couch inside the warm tree house and listened to the midday hum of insects outside, other childhood memories flooded his mind. Especially powerful was his remembrance of how, as a family, they would go to church every Sunday. It was small, immaculately white little building that somehow managed to fit in all the members of the tightly-knit congregation. Pastor Jones was a giant of a man who always spoke with an incongruously soft and gentle voice. Lee didn't remember the exact words of any of his sermons, but he did recall that he was never a fire and brimstone kind of preacher. His style was never to try to "scare the hell" out of his flock. Instead, he spoke of God's love and mercy and how, following His example, we as human beings needed to be understanding of one another's weaknesses and to live our lives with a disposition toward forgiveness and reconciliation.

Of course, in the many intervening years, Lee had drifted away from that simple proposition. He began to hold grudges and to become judgmental, not only about other people, but most often about himself. He'd beat himself up mentally and always be his own worst critic. In fact, that was one of the things that he and Rose had been arguing about lately. She told him that he put too much pressure on himself to always try to be perfect. When she would say that, Lee would take it as an insult, because he perceived it as a criticism of his treasured role as a provider.

But maybe she didn't mean it that way at all? Maybe because she loves me and hates to see me always worrying all the time and never showing even the slightest sign of weakness? In his mind, Lee answered his own question. It was indeed true. He never showed his wife, or anybody else for that matter, any indication of even the hint of vulnerability. It was one thing to set high standards, quite another to make it the focal point of his life. Was this the kind of man that he was meant to be? Was this the kind of life he was destined to live?

Lee eventually decided that it was time to climb down from the tree house and return to the trail. With the sunshine trickling through the thick canopy of leaves, he was walking along when the angel appeared to him walking down another path nearby. "I meant for you to remember who you are," said the Angel of Promise, "not worn out memories that fill us with good and bad experiences you may or may not like. Come over here, Lee, to walk my path. I want you to remember who you are. Go deep into your memories, Lee. You can do it."

For a moment, Lee had no idea what the angel was talking about. So he went within himself to find out what the angel was talking about with him. There was an answer, that much he knew. But he also knew that it could only be found within himself, not from any outside thing.

Lee took a deep breath and tried to forget his memories of "what" he was and remember "who" he was. All of the musing that he had done inside the tree house had only scratched the surface, he now realized. He recalled the memory he had not long ago in a dream of him returning to his own birth. Lee remembered moving through the womb of his imaginative perception of his birth to the moment just before he took physical form. He floated into and through the heavens and the stars and the vast galaxies of space within the universe. Lee could even remember where he had come from at one point.

He could see in the distance a small yellow light whose rays guided him to the center of this great light. He was surrounded by warmth, peace, and the feeling of love. Lee came alive within himself and felt the innocence of living life as though it was for the first time. He was gaining the capacity to live in the moment and really focus on it. The more he did this, the more peaceful and peace filled he became. His body would tingle just like the meditations he did years ago in a healing group.

Once again he heard the voice of the angel. "Now you're getting it," he said with a broad smile and in a soothing, calm tone.

Lee continued to focus, looking deep within himself where he now understood he would find all of the answers that he sought.

"You are getting there," the angel said, encouraging him to dive down even deeper into himself.

In the center of these energetic fluctuations was a stillness that felt like a womb like state of being. It was quite similar to the feeling he had in his mother's womb. It was a place he felt completely safe and cared for from every direction of his world. "That's it! That's it, Lee! You are there!"

"I see. Now, I see what you mean, Promise. This is who I am. This is what you want me to remember, isn't it?"

"Yes, Lee, this is what I want you to remember. Sometimes we have to leave the path we are on and take another one to remember who we are. All things are new to us and our ability to utilize the resources inside us to survive and thrive enables us to bring forth our spiritual qualities of existence to help us feel safe and strong in the world we live."

Lee was so enamored by this experience that he did not notice that Promise was no longer beside him, and how he had walked into the woods alone. Lee couldn't believe what had just happened to him. He was able to return to his birth point and realize the most powerful part of who he was lay in his innocence and trust in the world to create his life with the assurance of love. What was most amazing was that this truth had been inside of him all along. It was like a seed that had lain dormant all winter, now bursting with life when first kissed by the warmth of the springtime sun.

Lee spent the rest of his day touching and feeling the energy of the plants all around him and recalling his womb like state of being in his mother's womb. He now knew beyond the shadow of a doubt that he was not alone and that in fact he was connected to a vast and boundless universe that cared for him. He felt blessed, known, loved, and wanted. For the first time in years, Lee could move through the day with an awareness of who he was without the pressure of fulfilling an identity of what he or others thought he should be.

What a liberating experience! Lee felt exhilarated by this newfound freedom. How did he ever live without it? Life would be unbearable, in fact, if he ever had to go back to the old way he had been living. That would be a living hell — not really living at all. Thankfully, there was no reason to return to those old ways. Lee knew that what had just taken place would change him forever. There would be no turning back. They say that, once you learn, you never forget how to ride a bicycle. Now Lee knew that he would never forget how to truly live.

The next morning, Lee took a walk even deeper into the valley. He began to venture into territory he knew only a little of from the stories that his Grandpa had shared with him. Grandpa had always told him that the valley being a place where angels feared to walk. Perhaps it had something to do with the wild and aggressive animals in the valley below. Whatever it might be, Lee knew that he could not allow fear to keep him from his explorations.

Now, as he walked deeper and deeper into that valley he felt as though something was following him, but he could not figure out why he was having this feeling. He heard a few twigs crack around him and passed it off as probably nothing but some falling limbs. Then, he heard a growl sort of like a dog, but much more fearsome. Lee walked into an opening in the woods and found himself surrounded by an angry, snarling pack of wolves. Or were they really? Maybe they just looked that way because they were being protective of their own territory.

Lee's mind flashed back to the night that the intruder had broken into his home. Had he now broken into these wolves' home? Were they viewing him as the intruder? He needed to let them know that his intentions were not hostile and his purpose was not to steal anything or to hurt any of them. He noticed that some of the wolves were much smaller than the others, obviously cubs. He thought of his own children and how protective he was of them. It was an instinct of nature, and he knew that he had more in common with these wild animals than he ever could have imagined. Instead of fear, Lee experienced a sense of profound kinship with them.

Lee knew that he had no escape route and the wolves could beat him back to the cabin if he ran, so he simply started to walk slowly and purposefully without fear further into the woods ahead of him. The wolves followed him for miles curiously wondering why a man would go so deep into the woods and not fear being attacked. Lee came upon a stream and decided to sit by the water and meditate. He meditated for some time and came out of his meditation to find that not a single wolf was near him. He dipped some water out of the stream, filled his canteen, and made his way back to the cabin before night-fall.

Lee could only be amazed in disbelief of what had happened that day. *Could it be that being still and knowing you are protected and cared for releases us from the fear of being attacked in this world?* Lee wondered silently. The idea made so much sense, he almost felt foolish for never having realized it before.

During the night, Lee had another visit from Promise. "Did you see it? Did you see what happened today?" Lee asked the angel with much excitement. He sounded like a kid who has made a remarkable discovery and can't wait to share it with his parents or for that matter with anyone else who would listen to him.

"I did see it," Promise said, "and I was proud of how you handled yourself out there."

Suddenly thinking about the danger that he had been in, at least potentially, Lee sounded slightly bitter and asked, "Why didn't you come in to protect me? I could have been killed out there."

"I didn't have to," Promise replied, his tone calm as always and not the least bit defensive. "You realized who you really are and had just as much power as I did in that moment. Your innocence and willingness to trust the world around you much like you did in your mother's womb is so powerful that even the greatest of Kings and Queens stop everything they are doing to honor you."

Filled with new insight, Lee said, "This power you speak of is not what the world teaches us, is it?"

"Correct," said Promise, obviously pleased with Lee's gradually evolving enlightenment. "Humanity seeks to control what cannot be and have dominion over it. If this were the case, our world would be in much trouble. Everyone would seek power over one another and end up destroying each other in the process. Real power is to come to the point when you realize you are not able to hurt another without hurting yourself in the process."

"Tell me what you mean," said Lee.

"To hurt another being would disturb the connection you have been feeling the last few days with everything around you," Promise patiently explained. "This disturbance moves you into paths that take you out of your feeling totally cared for and safe. It then becomes a fight for survival and no one wins. There is a winner and a loser every time. Even the winner is the loser because this loss of connection to a fellow creature in soulfulness has been damaged."

"Ok, I get it now," said Lee. "This sure isn't what the world teaches us. How can we have traveled so long down a path that takes us away from our authentic love for one another?"

Lee began to think of the times in life he had measured himself against his brother, sister, wife, children, and friends. Each of these attempts are paths that lead to separation, anger, and even death. A great sorrow swept over him as he realized the utter folly and futility of the way that he had been living. How it had made him inadvertently harm those whom he loved. He knew that it was also harming himself. It was drawing him away from being the person that he had always felt he was meant to be. He resolved right then and there to never again look at life as merely some kind of a struggle to survive. Promise was right. It was a struggle destined to have a tragic outcome for all who engaged in it.

Lost in thought, Lee was now getting his days and nights mixed up. This whole experience in the woods was mystical enough without losing track of time as well. "Is this what you are asking me to do?" Lee wanted to know.

Promise confirmed for him that losing track of time is a good thing to do at times. "We live in a world measured by time. We measure everything. Sometimes, we need to relax and allow life to draw us into its essence."

Like every single word that Promise had spoken to him, Lee knew that this was rich in truth. "I know. I know," he said. "I need to relax at times. I tend to measure my success in living by those around me. I believe I have to do better than others to feel good about myself. You have taught me today to let go and let the creative order of my being reveal to me that there is no one greater or lesser than another. Being cognizant of that changes everything. Thank you, Promise."

"You are almost there, Lee."

"I'm not sure what you mean, Promise. I thought I have been fulfilling my promise to remember who I am these last few days."

"Lee, you have one more step to take before you can realize this part of who you are. Your name."

"Ok," Lee said, surprised. Every new revelation seemed to lead to new mystery. "What about my name?" he asked.

"To remember who you are is to remember your spirit name before you were labeled and defined as Lee," the angel responded, the very sound of his voice somehow conveying wisdom. "What is your spirit name?" he asked.

Lee thought for a long time about his spirit name. It was, as far as he could remember at least, the first time in his life that he had even heard of the concept. He racked his brain, but could not find an answer. Lee meditated upon it some more. Still nothing. When he was about to give up he heard in a still small voice, "I Am. I exist, therefore, I Am."

It was as though a bright light had shone within his soul.

"You got it," the angel said. "You are 'The Great I Am.' You always have been and always will be. This is enough for today. I will see you again, Lee."

"Thank you, Promise."

A Glimpse into Glory

"*What do you think? Do you think he is getting it?*" *Promise asked these questions to the elder angel.*

"*He is remembering who he is, but now, he needs to re-member himself as a heavenly being of light,*" *the elder angel replied.*

Lee's angel asked, "How can I get him to the point of reconnecting his identity with his most authentic self?"

The elder angel proclaimed. "You will help Lee by guiding him through the other six promises he made to you at birth. Lee will become his most authentic self in all its glory when he embraces the 'fullness' of who he really is. He will then know wholeness again. To remember who we are is the foundation of entering into angelic realms of the heart and soul. Each promise is like a puzzle and will create a whole picture from the various parts of Lee's personality he reclaims along the paths he is taking on the mountain. You must remember, Lee did not ask you to help him become anything more than what he thinks he is at present, but his soul longs for someone to show him his destiny."

The elder angel went on to say, "Just establish a relationship with Lee and allow his curiosity to deepen his interest in you. The deeper Lee enters into your divine presence, the deeper he will enter into the gates of heaven itself. Allow Lee to move into insight. When he is able to see within you what he cannot see about you, he will enter into the nature and inner visions of your soul. It will be Lee's probing inner curiosity that will enable him to realize that beyond form is a meeting of souls in the realm of the imagination and thought. Your words will become physical manifestations through the desires of the Lee's heart to be known."

Finally, the elder angel shared with Promise, "It will be through the desire of Lee's heart to remember with love how to communicate beyond words that the movement into a language of the soul becomes a possibility. And thus, Lee will be able to meet you in this place where all is known and no words to describe what cannot be will be understood. Here, Lee will know himself as he is truly known."

I Promise to Heal

Lee set out today to fish. When he was a teenager, he used to go fishing with his grandpa. On one fishing trip, Grandpa and Lee were in a two-man boat in Cadiz creek. This was a small creek in Western Kentucky. They were in a shaded area of the creek where cool water made for great fishing. Across the water was a snake swimming toward the boat. Lee was young and frightened. He did not know what to do. Grandpa sprang up, picked up a paddle in the boat, and hit the snake on its back as it was swimming toward the boat. The creature slithered away in the opposite direction. Lee always felt safe with Grandpa. It was just another day with his hero.

Lee pushed deeper into the valley where the big fish were known to be. On this day, he saw a bear hunting for fish downstream. It was unusual to see a bear this far south, Lee said to himself. The animal appeared to be a brown bear, though Lee wasn't familiar enough with bears to know for sure. He didn't seem to mind the human's presence, however, so Lee decided to simply focus on his own needs. He went about trying to find fish for his supper that night ignoring the bear downstream. He lost sight of this bear and believed he simply went away.

But he didn't. As Lee continued to fish, he noticed something was wrong and felt a huge presence behind him. When he turned to look around, the bear was standing on two feet. He lashed out and struck Lee across his stomach with his paw cutting him across his left arm.

Lee panicked, and had no idea what to do. He stood there with bright red blood dripping down his shirt. A wave of pain crashed over him, but only for an instant. Frozen still, Lee stared wide-eyed as the bear did something very strange after drawing blood. He watched Lee for a moment and then simply walked away.

Lee was far away from the nearest hospital, and no one was around to help him. He bled a great deal. Something inside Lee told him to hold his skin together and put pressure on it, which he did for the rest of the day. He tore his shirt off and wrapped it around his arm. The cut wasn't very deep and seemed to be a flesh wound. Lee was relieved and grateful that his experience was not as bad as he'd initially feared. Like most things in life, he realized as he repeated the incident in his mind repeatedly many times over the next few days, the fear itself had been far worse than what had actually happened to him.

In less than a week, Lee noticed that his skin was growing into itself. A scar was forming to remind Lee of this encounter with a bear. The shock soon wore off, and Lee was on the road to recovery. How is it that we heal? Lee pondered. How is it that our body knows what to do to heal? The answers to these questions were not as important to Lee as where this placed his attention. He was now realizing that he lived in a world that is healing and whole in nature. It is our thoughts of fear that scare us and scar us.

Lee realized that the bear was simply marking off his space and Lee was an intruder and a threat to the bear's survival. People are a lot like this, Lee thought. We claim space in the world and will fight anyone who tries to take what belongs to us in a fight to the death. It is the death of our souls that we really encounter. *The world does not belong to us. We belong to the world.*

"Where did that thought come from?" Lee asked out loud.

At that very moment, Promise walked out of the bushes and sat beside Lee. "Where were you?" Lee asked. "I could have been killed."

"But, you were not," Promise replied with a smile.

"I thought you protected humans," Lee wanted to know. He was more than a little disappointed that Promise seemingly had failed him.

The angel's expression let Lee know that this notion was untrue. He had been with him all this time and Lee still questioned himself. "Lee," Promise said. "I left you for a time, so you could know another part of yourself as a healer."

"Yeah, I thought I was going to die." Lee sounded like a small child complaining to his parents that everything in his life was not going exactly the way he wanted it to go. The circumstances were not conforming precisely to his own will. The universe was not complying with his demands. And small children throw temper tantrums when they don't get the exact answers that they want.

"But, you didn't die, did you?" Promise replied.

"No thanks to you," Lee said.

Promise just laughed. "You didn't die because you were born to regenerate yourself, Lee. You were born to recognize your true nature as a healer. You have spent a great deal of your time in these woods remembering who you are. You discovered that you are whole and a part of the whole and connected to what is whole. When the bear cut you, your ego thought you were going to die. You became frightened because you placed your identity of what you are as a body above who you are as a soul. In your calming down, you returned to your center...to your soul. When you recovered who you are as a soul that could not die, your ability to heal your own body from that place of awareness healed a separation that was never meant to occur."

"You are very good with words," Lee said to the angel, with an edge of skepticism in his voice. "How do I know these things to be true?"

"You will know them to be true from a place inside yourself that knows heaven to exist. Yes, I said heaven. Your perception of heaven to be a place outside of this existence keeps you from knowing your full potential as a healer. The instant you switch your thoughts from 'I am dying' to 'I will live' engaged a healing, a wholeness, a perception of heaven to fill your body with itself. The scar you have on your body is a reminder of the doubts you still have about your true nature. When you realize that heaven is not a place, you will move into a realization that you are a living presence of eternity given opportunities to accept your wholeness in physical form."

Lee's attention was riveted now.

Promise continued. "Do you remember, Lee, long ago when you stubbed your toe on a chair in the kitchen?"

Lee nodded. Though it was many years ago, decades actually, Lee remembered it as though it were yesterday.

"The pain took over all of your awareness," Promise explained. "In essence, you became filled with pain for a moment because you identified with it. Then, your dad came in and told you that it was too bad that your toe was hurting because he was going to get you an ice cream cone off the ice cream truck he could hear in the distance. I want you to notice what happened in that moment, Lee. Your attention shifted from a hurt toe to something much more pleasant in your mind. Your attention began to focus on drawing in an experience you would rather have. Literally, you filled yourself with a different energy besides the perception of pain. In so doing, there was no longer any more room for pain to exist in a peace filled awareness. Remember, Lee, wholeness and healing breathes in and through you and never comes from you or your experiences. The instant you embrace your true nature is the exact moment healing becomes more than a possibility."

Lee grew more and more interested in what Promise was saying about healing and asked him, "Why do we have to die?"

The angel just smiled and said, "Because you have forgotten how to live."

Lee wanted to know more. That answer was never going to be enough to satisfy his curiosity. The angel took a deep breath as though he was going back in time to call forth a memory he wished he could forget.

"In the beginning, man came into being as the most wonderful creature ever seen before in the history of time. Perfect in every way was the destiny of humanity. There were no needs or wants to fulfill and all was seen as good. One day, man began to focus his attention on what he was (body) and neglect to give thanks for who he was (soul). His attention grew to the point of forgetting his own essence. He forgot what fueled his very existence. Thus, the cycle of falling into a lower awareness in his attention level came into being. You see, all is energy. Our body is energy in motion. Everyone is created equal, but the attention of a man's focus will determine his destiny in ways even he cannot imagine."

Lee had been gazing into the angel's eyes as he spoke. Reading his thoughts, Promise said, "Yes, Lee. It can even determine the level of what humans call success or failure."

Lee responded, "Are you saying that if enough of us remember who we are and live from a place of wholeness and healing that life could be different?"

"It sure can, Lee. The problem is that so many people still doubt who they are and live from a place of lack and want; instead of realizing their unlimited potential. You are living in a time when the hands of time can no longer look back to ways life used to be. You have to move forward these days. Life is accelerating at a pace no one could have imagined centuries ago. The Internet has made us a global economy and extended our awareness of cultural and spiritual issues far beyond what most would have been comfortable with 100 years ago."

Promise was revealing things to Lee from a new perspective that he had never even considered before. He was eager to hear more.

"The time has come," said Promise, "for everyone to realize that everyone is in this thing called life together. Science has proved through quantum physics that the flight of a butterfly whose wings take flight into the sky effects the movements of time and space on the other end of the earth. Humanity is discovering what we angels knew long before we came to this point of living. Life is no longer predictable. Life is lived greatest when you live by the faith in what lies ahead will transform you into a greater awareness of what you are in the present moment. These are the people who will flourish in the years to come."

Lee pondered with much contemplation, and silence reigned between himself and Promise for a while. Then Lee said, "I now can see what you mean, Promise. In order for us to heal, we need to remember who we are and live our lives from that place of awareness and intention. Thus, creating a life lived from our most authentic self, and not, based on what we think we should be or what others think we should be. Somehow, it seems as though our survival of the human race will depend on this more than we know and even can know."

"So true, Lee," the angel said. Then he just smiled and turned around to walk in the woods again.

Lee was filled with so much hope and sorrow at the same time. He simply wanted to take in the rest of his day. He had no intentions or desires to accomplish anything. He just wanted to reflect on his latest conversation with Promise before going to sleep that night.

Getting It

"Lee is getting it," said Promise speaking to the elder angel.

The elder was encouraged by Lee's latest revelations. He said to Lee's angel, "Did you feel how deeply he was interested in what you said to him?"

"Yes, I did notice it. It felt as though he was completely inside me filling me with attentive openness."

The elder nodded his head. "He was inside you, and you were able to occupy the same space together as though there was only one of you."

"Yes, I could feel that from Lee."

The elder pondered all of this and then shared with his angel companion a moment of silence. Then, he broke the silence with these words, "You were both ONE in that moment. You shared an instant knowing. It was a knowing that has existed since the beginning of time. This eternal awareness is where all things come from - even healing. It is the knowing that all are ONE and all share eternity's gift of life that is eternal."

Promise listened further as the elder went on to say, "Healing is not something you and I discover. Healing discovers you. The process is not fully comprehended by any single entity in its entirety. We use our thoughts, feelings, and the movement of our soul to engage ourselves in it. Science uses medicine to help people get in a state of peace. This establishes an equilibrium in the body, so a person can center deep within themselves in order to find what is called peace. As a sense of peace is identified and embraced, it fills the body. It is the wholeness of one's soul that reveals a bridge to cross over from the demise of a body to living again."

Promise gathered himself and became aware of something he had not pondered before. In some ways, he realized his relationship with Lee goes both ways.

He needed to share enlightenment through the gift of a relationship with Lee in a giving and receiving encounter so that eternal love will move through him from the Source of all that ever has, is, and shall be.

I Promise to Hope

Today, Lee wanted to explore the rock formations on the paths known as The Garden of the Gods. He took along some rope because he wanted to climb them as well. When he reached the top of the hill at the Garden of the Gods, he couldn't help but take a deep breath to soak in the beauty of it all.

The mountainous hillside was utterly glorious. He understood why it was called the Garden of the Gods. Only a God could make something so beautiful, its magnificence unsurpassed in all of nature.

Lee could look for miles at the top of that mountain. There were a sea of trees filled with waves of green leaves. He was filled with energy and desire to climb down the peak of this mountain to a small cave below that led to a small path he could hike to a stream. He secured his rope on a tree and began to climb down the rock formation with much anticipation of entering the cave about 25 feet below him. About half way down this hillside, Lee's rope broke thrusting him into the air and helplessly down the mountain. Luckily, Lee found a tree limb to grab on the way down, but it was not secure and he could feel it beginning to break. Lee was not afraid to die, but he did not want to give up hope either.

As Lee hung on this tree limb, he wondered what was going to happen next. He began to say goodbye to the world, his family, and his friends. He said a brief prayer for God to take him home. And then, a white dove landed on this limb causing it to break further, thrusting Lee into a spiral motion that twisted his fall into the cave he was trying to reach. Lee was surprised to find himself safely landed in the cave below.

He could not have planned such an adventurous moment if he tried. It certainly was a story that he would share when he returned home to Ohio. It happened so fast. As Lee made his way through the small cave Grandpa told him about as a child, he was so grateful to be alive as he made his way to the other side of that hill.

His life could have been over in a flash. Who knows how long he would have lay at the bottom of this mountain before anyone would have found him. He could have been eaten by the wolves and the bears and no one would ever find him. Lee's sense of responsibility to how others would feel about his loss meant more to him than his own feelings. He had matured into becoming more soul than body on that day. His sense of connection to the well being of others' needs was sincere. Interestingly, Lee's favorite friends had this quality about them as well. His profound admiration of his closest friends gave him a glimpse into how others would see him when he eventually left Grandpa's cabin.

Lee had much love for his Grandpa. He really didn't know why, but he was getting an idea the longer he stayed in the mountains. Lee knew Grandpa shared his love of the mountains through stories. Now, he was feeling a deeper kinship to Grandpa in a way that transcended those stories he shared. He realized that Grandpa may not have been embellishing those stories like his mom and dad told him. He may have been telling a truth that could only be embraced as a fictional story by his listeners.

Lee was beginning to understand why Grandma admired Grandpa so much. She literally worshipped the ground he walked on. There was a spark in each of their eyes due to the deep gratitude they felt to be in a relationship with one another. Grandma liked to stay at home and gave Grandpa the freedom he needed to go to his cabin each summer to gather his thoughts. Grandma respected his privacy needs and looked forward each day for Grandpa's return to hear all the wonderful stories he had to share. After all, she knew she would be sharing the rest of that year together with the love of her life. They were constantly laughing and touching one another.

It was not a surprise to Lee to find Promise waiting for him at the cabin upon his return. Lee was exhausted emotionally, but he was glad to see this angel. "I almost died today," he said to the angel.

"What happened?" the angel inquired.

"My rope gave way down the mountain peak in the Garden of the Gods, and I dropped onto a limb that twisted and landed me in a cave. I then was able to walk through into the other side of the hill and make my way back to the cabin."

The angel asked with anticipation, "What happened as you held on to the limb?"

"I physically held on, but my mind and heart let go of living in case I fell to my grave. Somewhere in the middle of these thoughts, I held on to the hope that a part of me would not die."

"Interesting. Tell me more about your hope in a life beyond this one," Promise wanted to know.

"I simply had confidence that my life — the real me — would not die. I believed in that part of me, and it really didn't matter if my physical body would have died in that moment. I guess I valued my spiritual nature more than my physical one at that time."

Promise smiled as he turned to walk away. After taking a few steps, Promise turned around and said, "You found hope out there, Lee, in the face of death. It is always there, my friend. It is always there." The angel didn't stay as long on this visit. He seemed to be more grateful that Lee found hope, more so, than living through a near death experience.

Lee was beginning to understand why Grandpa went to his cabin every summer. His family had wondered several things about Grandpa's adventures on the mountain. Some of his family wondered if he was living a double life with another woman. Others simply thought he was a hermit at heart. But, Lee was beginning to realize that Grandpa went to the mountains to find his soul.

A Hope Abiding in Faith

T he Elder Angel spoke to Promise with much hope and enthusiasm on this visit to the angelic realms. "Lee has come a long way, Promise. He more than took a glimpse into his magnificent glory. He literally became fully divine while fully human with his recent experiences. His complete trust in a wisdom and a life beyond this one secured his path into spiritual realities forthcoming. He is well on his way to knowing himself as he truly is."

Promise said to the Elder Angel, "Did you see how his heart opened in the face of death? The man knew no fear."

"I did, Promise. I did. Promise, Lee just crossed a bridge inside himself that will allow him to become more spiritual in nature over the course of his remaining lifetime. When a man is able to see into a world beyond his own physical body, his connection to Eternal Truths will no longer enable him to define himself as a separate entity."

Promise said to the Elder Angel, "How must I relate to him now?"

The Elder pondered for a moment before saying, "He is no longer your student. Lee is now your friend. As Lee goes deeper into the essence of his being he will encounter wisdom and power that is just as great as your own, Promise. Give him space and the freedom to experience the expressions of his own power. Allow his awareness to expand beyond his own perceived limitations and enter into Unity Consciousness."

Promise realized that Lee was on a journey that no longer required his interventions. He knew that Lee presently had the capacity to make his way through the world as one able to manifest his desires to be known and to know on the level of soul. Promise knew that one thing was missing in his relationship with Lee. Promise knew that he needed to reveal to Lee the one promise he made to Lee at birth to fulfill his own destiny. For this reason, Promise awaited the next encounters with Lee to enjoy witnessing his unfolding grace reveal the beauty of his own essence.

8

I Promise to be Grateful

It had been about three months since Lee had seen another human being. He was getting lonely and wanted a companion to be with him. As he was taking a morning stroll through the woods, Lee heard a noise. It followed him through the woods much like the wolves did a little over a month ago. He decided that he was too far from the cabin to run back for shelter, so he simply tried to enjoy every minute in those woods without any fear that he might have.

He collected a few blackberries to take back with him for dinner and enjoyed the sights and sounds of nature all around him. He heard it again. Lee turned this time toward the noise behind him and said, "Show yourself."

Out of the bushes jumped a golden retriever. It had a collar on it and a name. "Grateful" was engraved on the collar. What a name, Lee said to himself, but an appropriate one. The dog didn't seem to have anyone looking for him and appeared to be lost and in need of a friend. Grateful followed Lee home to the cabin and stayed by his side for days and nights. The two of them became good pals. Grateful was very good at pointing out strange noises from the woods that came close to him and Lee. He was a good companion. He followed Lee everywhere.

Grateful was very dirty from spending time in the woods with no owner to care for him, so Lee took him to the stream and cleaned him up. It was not easy and Grateful was hard to hold onto. It took Lee holding Grateful tight and jumping into the water with him to get him clean. Lee laughed and couldn't remember a time when he had laughed so much in his life. This dog was bringing much joy to him.

Grateful was a good protector and alerted Lee when danger was near. He barked at a snake on one of the trails and just in time to because Lee was about to step on a copperhead that could have poisoned him. Lee grew more and more fond of his new-found friend.

Promise did not come around during this time. It was as though Lee had found a companion to fulfill much of his comfort needs and giving him space to do so. Lee would play fetch with Grateful, hide and seek, and many other made up games that brought the child out of him. Grateful was teaching Lee to have fun with life.

One day, Lee and Grateful took a walk into the valley. Lee had not been there in a long time and the fish were much bigger in the lowland streams. He felt safer to go with Grateful. He was not alone, so they took off one morning to catch the big fish. Lee wanted to share a big meal with Grateful that night.

When they reached the stream in the valley, Grateful dipped in his head and pulled out a huge trout. "You show off," Lee said. "You just had to catch the first fish." Lee took his spear and plunged it into the water and caught the second fish, and then another was caught soon after that one. They had three huge fish to take home and eat. It was more than enough for both of them, so they began to make their way home to the cabin.

On the way home, Lee began to feel the presence of a strange feeling surrounding him. Grateful was more alert as well and jumpy. When they reached the top of the hill near the cabin, the door was open and two wolves walked out to greet them. Then, there were three more wolves behind them. Grateful began to growl and Lee was aware that these wolves must have been growing in their confidence to eventually confront him again. This time, the wolves were not so curious. They were angry. It was as though they were protecting their land.

One of the wolves attempted to bite Lee from behind, but Lee was able to fend him off with his spear. Grateful drew in close to Lee to protect and be protected. Both were willing to give their life for one another at this point. Lee didn't want to be hurt, but he worried more for Grateful than himself. This allowed him to draw in much strength inside himself.

Another wolf lunged toward Grateful, and Lee caught it in the neck with his spear. It whimpered for a time and took its last breath as the other wolves stood and watched. There was a silence in all the woods at that moment. It was as though the world stopped to find out who would make the next move. The four wolves circled Lee and Grateful and paced around them looking for weakness. Lee was able to wound two more wolves who attempted to attack him. Grateful bit another's ear off in a single bite. And then, the leader of the pack had enough. He lunged forward for the kill. Lee had his back turned and didn't see what was coming. Grateful jumped into the air with the force of a mighty lion protecting its cubs and the fight was on. Lee held the other wolves back with his spear and could only watch and hope. The wolf was much stronger than Grateful, and eventually, took him down biting into the jugular vein in his neck. It was a mortal blow.

The wolves had proved their point and moved on as Lee kneeled before his new-found friend and cried. He gently rubbed his head, picked him up, and took him to the cabin. Grateful was going to bleed to death and Lee knew it. He tried to stop the bleeding with the shirt he had on his back. He took it off and wrapped it around his friend and held him until he died. It was a short death. Lee was glad that he didn't have to suffer much for such bravery.

Lee took Grateful to an opening near the cabin and buried him close by. He took a couple of rocks and used them as a headstone. He sat there for hours and just cried. After a day of mourning, Promise showed once again.

"Why so much violence in a peaceful world?" Lee shouted.

"You live in a world where people seek to control what cannot be, Lee. People think there is lack, so they protect what is believed to belong to themselves. In reality, there is more than enough for us all. Greed, anger, and dominance destroys people. If people only knew that life is meant to fulfill our potential in love, it would be a different place."

The Giving of Life for the Sake of Another

P romise looked puzzled when he spoke to the Elder Angel about what happened to Grateful. "I thought we sent Grateful to Lee to protect Lee from the forces of evil that were about to surround him and devour Lee's good nature?"

"We did, Promise," the Elder explained further. "I sent Grateful to companion Lee during his most trying time in the forest because he felt alone. Lee was beginning to question the growth he had made in spirit all because he felt alone. He was beginning to focus in on his own power and did not realize the unlimited *forces of spirit that had sustained him to that given point in time. I wanted Lee to know that service and love for another being reveals a hidden strength like no other path on earth. When people feel down and begin to lose emotional energy and trust in the joy of living, there is no greater way to gain strength again than to love another through acts of service."*

Promise took it all in as the Elder continued to share why Lee's most recent events just happened. "You see, people are the most vulnerable when they feel they are alone in the universe. The do not realize that the power within them is greater than the perception of external realities that come and go. Lee needed to know that the love and respect for life moving in and through him can and will sustain him through any loss that comes his way. When Lee entered into the moment whereby he was willing to give his life for a friend, he entered into tremendous power. His love for Grateful became his opportunity to discover a willingness to love another being greater than himself.

"You see, Promise, this movement of his soul into the realm of nobility enabled Lee to uncover a strength greater than his own limited self serving needs that lie within his ego. Lee encountered the face of death this

time allowing him to know love is greater than fear. In the exact moment Lee discovered that love was greater than fear, he became a living breathing force of nature. Lee was able to draw in universal strength into his being. His unshakable faith in love for another's safety overcame any fears he had of his own demise. This movement from self-centered awareness to life-centered awareness freed Lee from any fear he may face in the future."

Promise listened as the Elder spoke on, "Lee entered into a sacred pact with Grateful he will never forget. He loved Grateful enough to give his own love and his own life in order that his companion could live. Although his relationship with Grateful did not turn out the way Lee wanted it to, he moved into a place of willingness inside him to become grateful for what he had been given. A true sign of gratefulness comes to those who live in the world realizing they are more than what can be seen. In so doing, Lee became what he was seeking in 'the Spirit of Gratefulness' he found in this dog who came to him by his willingness to give his life for it."

I Promise to Grow

L ee told Promise he needed time alone. The angel could tell that Lee had much on his mind, so he left him for a time. Lee recalled memories of anger, greed, and dominance not liking what he saw. Yet, Lee was able to remember some great moments when he was altruistic in his life. He remembered a time in his life when he volunteered to go to a nursing home to spend time with an elderly woman. This woman shared many insights with him through her stories that she shared with him. The elderly are natural teachers of wisdom, Lee thought. Their experiences are reflected moments in tranquility that have deepened into their soul over time. From that time on, Lee spent a great deal of time with the elderly. He even found a job working with the elderly. For years, he worked with dying patients and watched the terrible emotional separation that loss brings to families in Hospice Care.

Over the years, Lee had watched a great number of elderly people become more gentle and forgiving toward the end of their life. He noticed that most of them became much more unconditional in the sharing of their stories about themselves and others. It was as though they no longer took themselves so seriously and finally realized their growth over the years.

Lee remembered a wonderful book that he had read over the years while he had been taking care of the elderly titled, "What the Dying Teach Us: Lessons on Living." In it, the author describes how dying people teach us to live. Each story is a reflection on a dying person's ability to teach us how to live in soul near their passing. Lee felt the same way over the years. He believed there was much to learn from those entering into their 2nd birth. It was as though their passing extended his perception of the world and living in eternal awareness.

Lee knew that dying people have little to lose in sharing their insights without holding anything back. It was as though they had no fear to be real. Lee admired this quality in the elderly and to this day found much courage in being himself with little fear of what others think of him. In fact, Lee had noticed over the years that his willingness to be honest about himself and others had helped him become more authentic and grow into incredible character. It was as though it was a silent promise made between himself and the elderly in living life with boldness and unconditional love.

After a couple of hours, Promise returned to Lee. "Have you had enough time to yourself?" asked the angel.

"Yeah," Lee said. "I could use some company now."

Lee was emotionally exhausted. He had been through a lot in the last three days and Promise was much comfort to him just sitting close by and listening. Lee broke the silence and said to Promise, "One of the things I noticed over the years is how mature people enjoyed a great deal of silence." The angel just smiled. "I wonder if there is so much for them to reflect on that the need to talk is silenced by their need to embrace their past and their soul," said Lee.

Promise just sat and smiled as Lee continued to talk. "I have spent a great deal of my time filling my head with information and little time analyzing its truths. This must be why the elderly are so wise. There are really just a few truths we need to know, and the rest are fillers of time because of our fear of losing touch with the outside world."

The angel nodded affirmatively.

Lee went on to say, "I am going to spend more time simplifying my life. I am going to focus on the things I really know I can do to bring good into the world and let everyone else handle their own lives. I am tired of measuring myself to my neighbor and friends as though my self-esteem and self-worth are tied to it. It is time for me to be me. I want to fulfill the me I came to be." Lee's voice sounded so confident as he said these words. They came from a place inside him rooted in such certainty that nothing or no one could alter him from being his true self.

Promise laughed and said to Lee, "You do this and some may think you are crazy."

Lee went on to say, "I know, but at least I will have my self-confidence back and no longer will I be controlled by others' need to see me in ways that they want to see me."

Lee felt so free in saying this to Promise. For the first time in years, he felt as though he had a focus. It was a clear focus that needed no one to affirm him. He was so certain of this he felt his life and existence fill up inside him. From this moment forward, Lee recognized that the torch had been passed to him from his elders. It was his turn to become more reflective and obtain inner wisdom before he died.

Inner Growth

Promise spoke to the elder in a rather proud voice. *"Lee is on his journey home."*

"Yes, the elder affirmed. Lee has realized that the true meaning of self-esteem and self-worth lies in what he thinks and feels about his own self. People get this all confused, Promise. They define self-esteem and self-worth the wrong way. You could say that most people rely on other-esteem and other-worth to define themselves; instead of the other way around."

"Yes, why do people do this to themselves?"

The elder stated, "It is easier to define the boundaries of living based on realities that can be measured. This limiting view of oneself creates a path that requires little faith beyond oneself. People get the feeling that they are in control of their own life and feel safe."

Promised listened further as the elder went into deep reflection as though he was remembering events of human experiences since the beginning of humanity.

Promise interrupted. "This keeps people from realizing who they really are."

"Indeed it does," the elder proclaimed. "Because of this, humanity has paid a huge sacrifice for such behavior, Promise."

"What do you mean?" Promise wanted to know.

"People begin a path that will certainly lead to their downfall. They begin a journey into building a life around them to protect themselves from knowing the true meaning of creating their lives from a higher awareness of what life can be for themselves. Thus, they will never know the creative force that breathed their life into existence as the same force of living that will lead them into unlimited potential and unlimited power."

The elder looked Promise in the eyes and said to him, "Lee has found the way home. He has found the true meaning of living in the world knowing he is no longer defined by it. This will give Lee the potential to allow his true essence to flow through him and not from him. He will now know true power, true self-worth, and true self-esteem. He will know himself as Spirit."

I Promise to Live in Wholeness

L ee was starting to understand something about living. He noticed that at the beginning of life and at the end there was so much grace and unconditional love. He asked Promise, "How can I know wholeness?"

The angel was glad he asked this question because only a mature person would actually be able to want and understand it. "First of all, no single human being is perfect. They are in constant human evolution and growth into remembering who they really are. It takes a childlike faith or the experience of many years to live life in wholeness."

He went on to say that wholeness is the ability to get back up when you take a fall in life. It is also the ability to laugh and give grace to your perceived failures. "You once knew how to do this, Lee," said Promise.

Lee found these words to be intriguing. "What do you mean by *perceived failures*?" he asked.

"When you come to this earth, Lee, you are going to experience a fall into what you consider a failure. This is not so. You come from a much greater experience of your identity than what you place on yourself through judgments and labels that serve to limit yourself. Your *perceived failures* are nothing more than opportunities for you to know grace, forgiveness, and unconditional love. This understanding of unconditioned grace is your attempt to identify with your true nature. It is your ability to reach inside yourself and come to know you have the ability to connect with something much greater than your physical identification of what you think you are. In so doing, this higher elevation of your thoughts into a knowing or shall I really say a remembering of who you really are is a choice you make within yourself.

Promise spoke to Lee with much more than just great knowledge and wisdom, the abundance of which was in itself astounding. Even more compelling to Lee, however, was the way on which this heavenly being communicated to him with a lovingness unlike anything that had ever blessed his ears before. There was a timelessness, a hint of eternity embedded deep within every syllable that the angel spoke to him. "This shift in your conscious awareness to connect with the innocence you were born into the world with as an infant is a returning to your childlike innocence," Promise said. "It has enough power to free you from any notion of what you have become in your own mind. Your heart will embrace a love not bound by the limits created on this earth."

Lee watched Promise with rapt attention as he spoke and noticed that the angel seemed to speak as though he was drawing his words from a place beyond space and time. He seemed to be reaching into eternity and creating a life on earth through his spoken words. They were words of love and made Lee feel good inside. It was as though Lee was being filled with wisdom that he could no longer deny to be true. This wisdom resonated within Lee as words he was familiar with from a long time ago. All that he had forgotten now came rushing back to him like a great torrent of rain showered upon an expectant field that had been parched and dying without its life-giving essence. Lee drank it all in like a man who had been wandering in the desert.

Lee closed his eyes and a vision came to him. He imagined himself without a body and a mind being aware of all that was around him. It was as though he was completely surrounded by this energy. He was not standing on the ground in this vision nor had a body, and he felt completely safe. There was not even a close identification with or need for a body to sustain him in this vision. He felt connected to everything without the fear of losing his own personal identification with what he had learned to inhabit as a child called a body. Lee never felt so whole in his life. He was free from the pushing and pulling of his mind and heart to do and be anything. It was good enough for him to just exist in this vision and know he always would be alive in it forever. The experience infused new meaning into the simple word "life."

Promise tapped Lee on the shoulder and wore a knowing smile upon his face as he asked, "Where did you go?"

"Nowhere," Lee said. "I mean. I was here, but I was everywhere at the same time."

The angel chuckled. "Your face glowed as though you were flying across the universe without any struggle whatsoever."

"It felt that way," Lee acknowledged. "It felt that way."

Lee and the angel sat there in front of the cabin with a small bonfire to warm them as the night's air drew near. Lee felt as though he was limitless with his words and ability to understand life in a way he had not been able to do so before. He listened to the angel go on and on about unconditional love that is available to us all. Lee listened to Promise as though every word that came out of his mouth were words raining down from Heaven. Lee grew to love this angel as a long lost friend helping him to love and understand himself more fully.

Unlimited Wholeness

The elder spoke to Promise immediately when they met this time. *"Did you see him glow?"*

"Yes, I did," said Promise. *"He lit up the heavens with his love,"* Promise went on to say.

"He was like a child, Promise" the elder retorted.

"He brought his soul forward from the depths of his life experience as an infant," Promise said with enthusiasm.

The elder looked deep into Promise's eyes and said, "He remembered his birthright. He remembered the days when no words were needed between him and his parents to speak the language of love. The language of the soul describes what cannot be defined and words are not really enough to embrace a love that transcends even the need for it. It is the language of the heart that takes people into a place where unconditional love can be shared and people can be known as they are truly known."

The elder left Promise with a final teaching. He went on to say, "Lee has crossed into the area many angels do not dare to tread. It is the land of wholeness and purity much like what was known in the beginning of time itself. This is the land of God's creative order. You must tread lightly upon such Holy Ground for this is the heart of creation itself, if not, the heart of God. Know your place, my friend, and allow your heart to expand into unlimited potential."

I Promise to Live in Abundance

The next morning, Lee felt so refreshed that he took a walk deeper into the woods to the other side of the valley. He found a trail that led up another mountainside near the Garden of the Gods. He climbed about halfway up the hillside and began to notice many wildflowers along the way. They were yellow, pink, and white. Much more color, Lee said to himself, on this side of the mountain.

As Lee walked farther up the trail, he noticed a buzzing sound that became louder each step of the way. Occasionally, a honey-bee would zip past by him. He said to himself that many bees probably seek out this place to draw from the nectar the wildflowers provide. Soon he came to an opening, it was an open field with trees here and there filled with bee hives and bees buzzing in and out of the trunk of these trees. Lee could smell the fresh hot honey being processed by the bees. Their work was steady and everyone seemed to have a job to fulfill. There wasn't a single bee laying around without a job to do.

In the center of these bees' activities were golden combs of honey that looked like golden coins glistening in the sun's rays of light. This field of golden honey created a glow that reached from the heavens above to the earth below with one single ray of light. Lee was filled with a level of energy that made him feel light on his feet. It was as though he was walking on air and being sustained by an energy greater than himself.

Lee was fascinated by these bees to the point that he simply stood and admired their work in progress. There was much energy and focus coming from that area of the mountain. Lee noticed his thoughts get lost in the purposeful fulfillment of the life these bees seemed to have. Each bee worked to secure the enhancement of the queen bee whose purpose in living was to secure more golden honey for them to live. This not only sustained the life of the bees, but it sustained the survival of their species as well.

Lee could understand this type of living, for he lived in a similar way. He worked to bring in money for the survival of his family and to make his queen bee (wife) happy. It wasn't that he was made to do so by his family. Lee had chosen to do so out of the desire to help his family survive beyond himself.

No bee seemed to go hungry for anything. Each flew out during the morning hours to find pollen that could be brought back to make honey. Others stayed behind to do what was necessary to prepare the hives for their return. Every bee had a chore to do. No one seemed to be laid off from their jobs because there was plenty to do around them.

Lee went on to think to himself that true abundance is knowing your life will be utilized for the betterment of society; rather than, lived selfishly to meet our own needs. How service to others reveals our character, and it reveals our soul. These bees have a great deal to teach us.

The business of the bees energized Lee. There was much life in this place. Everyone had a task to fulfill. It took Lee all day to make his way back to his cabin. In front of his cabin, Promise was there to greet him with some fresh fish cooking over an open fire. "Where did you go today?" said Promise.

"I walked over to the other mountain near this one and saw a field of bees. I was amazed at the organizational skills of these bees, and how, each one had a job to do."

"Tell me more," Promise wanted to know.

Lee went on to say, "I noticed these bees seemed to be filled with something. It was a vision, a purpose, and a reason to live. It created endless energy for them. Something seemed to move them besides their physical bodies. It felt like energy."

"Yes," the angel retorted. "Yes, the bees were being filled with a focus upon a vision that caused them to have an abundance of energy that never ends," Lee added.

"This is the secret to living, my friend Lee. Fill your mind and your heart with a vision greater than seems possible at the moment and watch what happens. You will be given a pathless path into spirit allowing you to have energy and information flow through you, and not, from you. This is a feeling of unlimited energy and abundance that will carry you to your dream and your visions in life. When you are connected to it all, you will have unlimited energy and potential to drive you forward."

Lee was content. He seemed to realize a secret to living that had been with him all along. It was a secret because he did not take the time to recall his soul into the present and reflect on what brought him to this moment in time. He even realized that his life had simply evolved this way unconsciously. Now, Lee was determined to live his life purposefully and more abundantly. He realized there were not limits to what he envisioned anymore. He could see the world clearly now.

One Final Secret Revealed

The elder angel met Promise at Heaven's gate on this visit. "Promise, I believe your work with Lee has come to a place of fulfillment."

"I know," said Promise.

"He is on his way," the elder said in a soft and peaceful voice. He went on to say, "Promise, you still have one more thing to do with Lee."

"Oh yes, I do don't I," he said to the elder.

"Lee has been curious about you, Promise, since the day he met you. It is time to reveal yourself to him. It is the ultimate level of intimacy between a man and his angel. When you reveal to Lee who you are, he will know his true nature. In so doing, he will begin his journey *into the path of the angels. He will be able to help others along the way find faith, hope, and love. And know, the greatest of these is love."*

Promise turned from the elder with a determined focus inside himself to prepare himself for his final revelation to Lee. It was an inner feeling of joy and sorrow brewing inside of Promise. It was time to let his friend Lee go and find his own way. It was time for Lee to spread his own wings to fly.

"Before you go, Promise, there is a side of me I need to share with you."

"What do you mean?" Promise said.

The elder angel, known also as Rosa Lee said, "Tell my grandson that his grandmother and his grandfather are very proud of him."

Promise smiled as he walked away speaking to himself in a soft voice, "I always knew you had a strong feminine side to you."

The Road Home

It had been four months and Lee was starting to miss his wife. His heart began to pull him toward Ohio. They had been together for a long time now and their hearts had become one in many ways. Lee had been in the woods long enough to know that he had better follow his heart for it was his soul's path calling him to action.

Lee decided to go to the cave of crystals again to say goodbye. He had recovered much of his strength and remembered his true nature. Lee walked the path to the cave and each step seemed to be purposeful and attentive attention to his surroundings as it expanded his awareness like no other time in his life. When he reached the cave, Lee dove into the water. He swam through the opening near the bottom of the swimming hole and made his way into the cave of crystals.

Lee realized that something mystical was in this cave. It felt like he was in a womb that carried the spirit of eternity within it. As he entered a dark, distant part of the cave, Lee heard a voice. It was a familiar voice. A small light appeared and the light began to move closer and closer to Lee, illuminating the cave of crystals. Now there was no doubt about it. It was Grandpa.

Grandpa said to Lee, "My grandson. It is me. You have come to the cave of crystals guided by the circumstances of your life. Your father came to this cave when he was 40. I passed on the cabin keys to him at that time. When you go back to see your dad, he will pass on the keys to you I gave to him many years ago. You will need to know the code though. Say to your dad, 'We who have given faith.' He will then know to pass on those keys to your generation."

Overwhelmed with emotions, Lee said, "I'm not sure that I even belong here in this world anymore. I want to be where you are, Grandpa."

But the benevolent voice said, "You will someday pass through the cave of crystals, but it is not your time. You must go back and fulfill your destiny, Lee. You have much living to do before it is your time. Follow the wisdom you have gained here at the Garden of the Gods. Let it lead you into a life of abundance with unlimited possibilities that will lay at your feet. All you have to do is believe in yourself, trust the wisdom that created you, and fulfill the promises you made to your angel of promise the moment you were born."

Grandpa's light began to fade and Lee's heart sank. Yet it was a different kind of sadness than what he had felt at Grandpa's funeral. This feeling was far less gloomy because embedded within it was the certainty that this was not the last time he would see his grandpa.

Lee felt another strange feeling as well. This time Lee noticed that his grandpa's passing seemed to expand his own awareness. His awareness of Grandpa leaving him this time deepened Lee's soul. It was as though an eternal connection bonded Lee and Grandpa in a way death could not separate.

Lee was glad to see his grandpa again. It was a gift he would never forget. Lee felt more sad that he was getting ready to leave the Garden of the Gods than leaving Grandpa behind. Yet, his heart longed to be with his wife Rose again. Lee was feeling these things with much more intensity than before, and it was ok. He never felt more alive before in his life.

Later that morning, Lee began to pack his belongings for the ride to Kentucky. It was going to be good to see his family in Kentucky again. He knew the visit would do him good before he returned to Ohio. Lee spent an extra long time packing his clothes. It was like saying goodbye to an experience he did not want to end. The air was clear and fresh in the mountains. He would miss it.

When Lee put his belongings in the car, he went back to the cabin to say goodbye one last time to his experience in the mountains. He heard a sound like a distant echo say, "I'll be with you. I'll be with you." Lee had heard many sounds in the mountains, and this one was another simple reminder just how special this place really was. It did not sound like Grandpa's voice or the angel. It must have been the mountain itself, Lee thought to himself. A fascinating thought.

Lee walked back to the car to drive off and turned into the sun for just a moment. "No, it couldn't be," Lee said to himself. He thought he saw an angel hovering over him in the rays of the sun. Lee turned the key to his car and began to make his way down the mountain. Ahead was the old ferry to take him from the Illinois side to the Kentucky side near his folks' home. As Lee rode to the other side of this ferry, he climbed out of his car and walked to the railing, so he could look into the water. Lee had not looked at himself in some time. He had grown a beard. It was getting pretty long too. Lee had always been a clean-shaven man and wondered if his family would recognize him when he walked into their home.

Lee passed his old high school in Marion, Kentucky. He remembered many pleasant memories while going to that school. He used to play sports there, and had many friends still in town. When he drove up into his mom and dad's driveway, Lee was greeted with a smile and a hug from his mom and a traditional handshake from his dad. His sister and brother's family were there cooking hamburgers on the grill. Lee felt at home, but he could only stay a few days. He gave the cabin keys to dad and he just smiled. "Did you have a good time, Lee?"

"I did, Dad," and they both winked at each other as though sharing a long held secret passed on from Grandpa. Then, Lee gave his dad the keys to the cabin. That night, Lee had a talk with dad on the back porch.

"Son, how was your time in the cabin?"

"Great, Dad, I really needed it."

"I remember going there many years ago myself, Lee. It was a much needed visit. Do you have something for me, Lee?"

"Yes, I do, Dad. I was told to share with you a code, so you can give me the keys I gave you. Dad, I was told to say, 'We who have given faith.'"

"You must have found the keys to living in those hills, Lee."

"I did, Dad. I did."

At that time, Lee's dad handed him three rusty keys.

"I didn't receive and give you these keys, Dad."

"Yes you did, Lee."

"How can this be?" Lee said.

Lee's dad went on to say, "You received keys that you envisioned from the depths of your soul's need. I gave you three rusty keys. These keys did not open that cabin door. The lock on the door would be hard to open by now. It was the keys to your heart that opened the cabin door in the mountains."

"You mean, this was an imaginary trip?"

Dad smiled. "No, Lee, you were there, but the experiences you manifested came from your heart's desire to discover what you needed most. To you, these keys were made of gold because of the life it opened up for you. Life in those mountains were what you made it out to be; so it is in life."

"You're starting to sound like the angel I met on the mountain, Dad."

Lee looked at his dad much differently in that moment. It was as if Lee and his dad were transcending time and space and living in an other-worldly experience shared by two different times in history, and yet, only moments apart from one another infused by eternity.

Lee spent another day with his family in Kentucky and packed to leave for Ohio. He then spent the whole day driving. Along the way, he went over the memories he had in the mountains. He learned many things could be revealed to him if he would only open his heart to his surroundings and allow miracles to flow through him. Most of all, Lee appreciated how the art of allowing life to happen had a way of connecting him to all of life in an esoteric way. From this moment on, Lee was going to see the world differently. He realized that he could not be harmed or harm another without every living thing suffering as a result. Lee just wanted to do his part in the world and become the best he could be as a person, for he now knew it reflected his soul.

Lee arrived that night tired. His wife and family greeted him, but he wanted to spend more time alone with his wife Rose unpacking his belongings. It was a tender evening of greeting, touching, and gently getting used to being around one another. Their passion for one another was deeply felt in the heart and soul of their very existence. Rose and Lee had both entered into a level of care where only souls could embrace such an existence. "How was your trip, Lee?"

"It was nice, Rose, but it is good to be home with you."

"I'm glad," Rose said silently to herself. "It's been four long months without you, Lee."

"I know, I missed you too, Rose."

As they faced one another to kiss, the caress of Rose's breath long before Lee touched her lips created a sensation of anticipation like he had never known before. When their lips locked, they could not get enough and time stood still.

The bed had fresh sheets and a fragrance sprayed all over to give the feeling of being wanted and loved. Rose and Lee lay in bed that night talking to one another until they fell asleep sometime in the night. It didn't take long for Lee to go into a deep sleep. He found himself recalling those moments in the Garden of the Gods throughout the night. Just before Lee woke up the next day, he dove into the water and entered into the cave of crystals.

"Hello. Hello." Lee said, "Is it you?"

"Yes Lee, it is me."

"I guess, you will always be with me."

"Yes, I always have been and always will be with you, Lee."

"Ok, you promised me something on the mountain. You promised me that you would tell me who you are and the one promise you made to me at birth."

"I did, didn't I."

At that moment, the angel's presence began to lighten up the whole room in the cave of crystals. There were sparkles of every color known to man until the room became a single golden color. His wings spread wide when he opened them and hid behind his back when he closed them. It was almost more than Lee could take in at the time. Lee said, "What happened to you?"

"It is me, Lee. I came to you in human form so you would eventually accept me as I really am at a later time."

"I don't believe my eyes." Lee's eyes were astonished at the magnificence of his angel. For the first time in years,

Lee could see with incredible clarity. He could hear the slightest movement of the angel's wing brush through the air. It was like a symphony and like no other music he had heard in his lifetime.

"Tell me, what is the promise you made to me at birth?"

"Lee, I promised to love you always, and in, all ways."

"You mean, you would love me unconditionally no matter what?"

"Yes, I always have and I always will - eternally."

"I should have known this. I have always known I was loved at the core of my being. Ok, you promised me you would tell me your name and reveal who you are."

The angel just smiled and looked at Lee for a moment. His golden light became almost too bright for Lee to gaze into any longer. His light became so bright that the room became a single white glow. He wrapped his incredibly long wings around Lee's entire body. Lee could feel himself protected and strong at the same time. The angel blended into Lee and the two became one. At that moment, Lee's body was the golden light he came to know in the angel. Lee rose up from this deep sleep and shouted, "I get it! I get it!"

Acknowledgements

I want to thank Mike Valentino for his Editing talents on this project and his insights and direction on making this fictional novel come to completion. I want to thank my own Angel of Promise who guided me through this manuscript. Most of all, I want to thank God who makes all things possible under Heaven.

About the Author

S am Oliver has cared for the needs of the dying in palliative care for over 17 years. During that time, he has served as the Chair, and a, Co-Chair of the Hospice Ethics Committee at a Hospice Care Center in Northern Ohio. He has served several years as a State Continuing Education Chairperson for the Association of Professional Chaplains.

For well over a decade, Sam has been an active editorial review board member and contributing writer for Healing Ministry Journal, The Journal of Terminal Oncology, and The American Journal of Hospice and Palliative Care. He began his speaking about spiritual care over 15 years ago and continues to speak at public engagements on the local, national, and international levels. He has spoken at several college campuses and keynoted at several Hospice Conferences.

His first book of four, *What the Dying Teach Us: Lessons on Living,* is a Doubleday Book Club, One Spirit, and National Hospice and Palliative Care Organization selection. Sam's undergraduate study was at Georgetown College with a B.A. in Psychology. He received his Master of Divinity at The Southern Baptist Theological Seminary in Louisville, Kentucky, with an emphasis in the Pastor/Teacher track. In 2003, Sam Oliver finished his postgraduate certificate in Healthcare Ethics through Rush University in Chicago, Illinois.

Presently, Sam Oliver is a Chaplain and a Bereavement Counselor for a Hospice Care Center in New Hampshire. For more information on this author: www.pathintohealing.com

To order

Angel of Promise

and other books by Sam Oliver, go to:

www.pathintohealing.com

or send check or money order for $12.95
(+ $7 shipping and handling) to

Fideli Publishing
119 W. Morgan St.
Martinsville, IN 46151

Or to order with credit card over the phone call

888-343-3542

Reduced shipping rates and discounts available
for higher quantity orders, please call for details.

Breinigsville, PA USA
09 April 2010
235834BV00004B/2/P